World
Tales

Anansi the Banana Thief

An African–Caribbean tale told by
Anne Adeney

Illustrated by Yannick Robert

FRANKLIN WATTS
LONDON • SYDNEY

First published in 2010 by
Franklin Watts
338 Euston Road
London
NW1 3BH

Franklin Watts Australia
Level 17/207 Kent Street
Sydney
NSW 2000

Text © Anne Adeney 2010
Illustration © Yannick Robert 2010

A CIP catalogue record for this book is available
from the British Library.

ISBN 978 0 7496 9416 6 (hbk)
ISBN 978 0 7496 9422 7 (pbk)

Series Editor: Jackie Hamley
Editor: Melanie Palmer
Series Advisor: Catherine Glavina
Series Designer: Peter Scoulding

Printed in China

Franklin Watts is a division of
Hachette Children's Books,
an Hachette UK company.
www.hachette.co.uk

This tale comes from
West Africa. Can you
find this on a map?

One day, Monkey
went out shopping.

"I want to buy fish and some mangoes," he said. "What else do I need?"

"Bananas," said Anansi.
"You should buy lots of
bananas."

"Yes, I do need bananas, but I do not need your help," said Monkey.

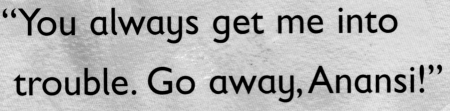

"You always get me into trouble. Go away, Anansi!"

7.90

15.40

4.70

7

But as Monkey was busy paying, Anansi took the bananas and ran off into the woods.

Monkey was scared. Lion lived in the woods, but he had to get his bananas back, so he followed Anansi.

Just then Monkey
heard a cry: "Help!"

Then Anansi appeared.
"My friend Lion is stuck in
this pit. I helped you buy
your food so you should
help me rescue Lion."

"But lions eat monkeys!"
cried Monkey.

Anansi threw Monkey's tail into the pit.

Lion grabbed the tail
with his teeth.

17

Anansi pulled Monkey ...

Monkey pulled his tail ...

And Lion was saved!
He was also hungry
and started eating
Monkey's tail.

"Help me, Anansi!"
cried Monkey.

"Lion! Aren't you going to say thank you?" asked Anansi.

"Thank you," said Lion.
As he opened his mouth,
Monkey's tail fell out.

Monkey ran off as fast as he could. Lion chased him.

Anansi took Monkey's food home. "A good morning's work," he smiled. "I do like bananas."

29

Puzzle 1

HELP!

Put these pictures in the correct order.
Now tell the story in your own words.
What different endings can you think of?

Puzzle 2

nervous   worried

horrible

crafty   caring

naughty

hungry   gentle

fierce

Choose the correct words for each character. Which words are incorrect? Turn over to find the answers.

Answers

Puzzle 1

The correct order is 1d, 2f, 3e, 4b, 5c, 6a

Puzzle 2

Monkey: the correct words are nervous, worried

The incorrect word is horrible

Anansi: the correct words are crafty, naughty

The incorrect word is caring

Lion: the correct words are fierce, hungry

The incorrect word is gentle

Look out for Leapfrog World Tales:

Chief Five Heads
ISBN 978 0 7496 8593 5*
ISBN 978 0 7496 8599 7

Baba Yaga
ISBN 978 0 7496 8594 2*
ISBN 978 0 7496 8600 0

Issun Boshi
ISBN 978 0 7496 8595 9*
ISBN 978 0 7496 8601 7

The Frog Emperor
ISBN 978 0 7496 8596 6*
ISBN 978 0 7496 8602 4

The Gold-Giving Snake
ISBN 978 0 7496 8597 3*
ISBN 978 0 7496 8603 1

The Bone Giant
ISBN 978 0 7496 8598 0*
ISBN 978 0 7496 8604 8

Bluebird and Coyote
ISBN 978 0 7496 9415 9*
ISBN 978 0 7496 9421 0

Anansi the Banana Thief
ISBN 978 0 7496 9416 6*
ISBN 978 0 7496 9422 7

Brer Rabbit and the Well
ISBN 978 0 7496 9417 3*
ISBN 978 0 7496 9423 4

Little Tiger and the Fire
ISBN 978 0 7496 9418 0*
ISBN 978 0 7496 9424 1

No Turtle Stew Today
ISBN 978 0 7496 9419 7*
ISBN 978 0 7496 9425 8

Too Many Webs for Anansi
ISBN 978 0 7496 9420 3*
ISBN 978 0 7496 9426 5

*hardback